NEUGEBAUER PRESS LONDON, BOSTON

COPYRIGHT © 1983, VERLAG NEUGEBAUER PRESS, SALZBURG, AUSTRIA
ORIGINAL TITLE: PHILIPP UND DIE KUNST
COPYRIGHT © 1983, ENGLISH EDITIONS, NEUGEBAUER PRESS U.S.A.INC., BOSTON
PUBLISHED IN U.S.A. BY NEUGEBAUER PRESS U.S.A.INC.,
DISTRIBUTION BY ALPHABET PRESS, BOSTON.
PUBLISHED IN U.K. BY NEUGEBAUER PRESS PUBLISHING LTD., LONDON.
DISTRIBUTION BY A&C BLACK, LONDON.
ALL RIGHTS RESERVED
PRINTED IN AUSTRIA
ISBN 0 907 234 25-9

HANNE TÜRK

MAX THE ARTLOVER

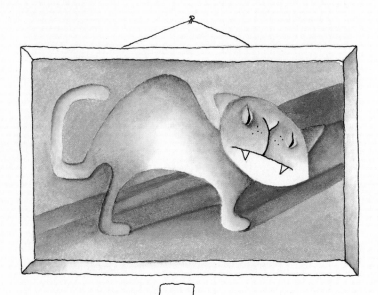